This SOCCER Coloring & Activity Workbook Belongs To:

____

The Champ

Written By: Carline Constant and Gregory Constant
Illustrated by: Leena Shariq

For information contact us online at: www.sprinklejoybooks.com

Summary:
The Champ captures the relationship between a boy with his grandpa in sports. Join Amari, his sister Aida, and Grandpa on their quest to turn Amari into a soccer champion who embraces the value of teamwork.

Subjects:
CYAC: 1. Soccer Sportsmanship - Juvenile Fiction. 2. Teamwork Sports – Fiction 3. Grandparents and Grandchild - Fiction 4. Boys and Girls Siblings – Fiction/Picture Book.
5. African American family - Realistic Fiction. 6. Champion Sports – Fiction. 7. Book For Boys and Girls - Picture books.

Identifiers:
Paperback ISBN # 979-8-9865546-0-0
Hardcover ISBN# 979-8-9865546-1-7
eBook ISBN # 979-8-9865546-0-0
Workbook ISBN # 979-8-9865546-2-4

Library of Congress Control Number: 2022916166
LCCN Imprint: Sprinkle Joy Publishing,
Brooklyn, New York

10987654321
Printed in the United States of America
First Edition: December 2022

Semi Realistic Art Style
For Ages 5-12

Thanks to God for everything.

For all young at heart!

Winning in sports requires teamwork.

For my sons, Gregory, Anthony and Andy.

-Carline Constant

For all aspiring athletes around the world.

-Gregory Constant

Dedicated to my papa, my mamma, my sisters and my brother for their words of encouragement and absolute support in this

journey of mine.

-Leena Shariq (illustrator)

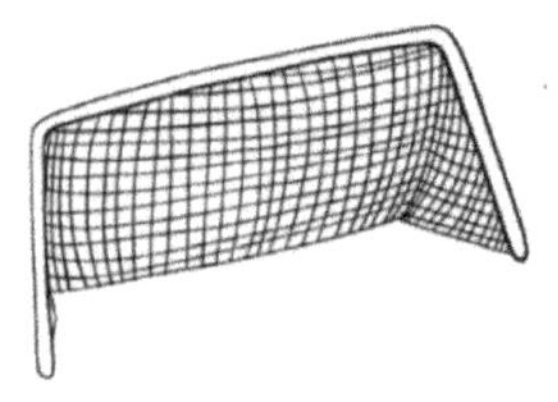

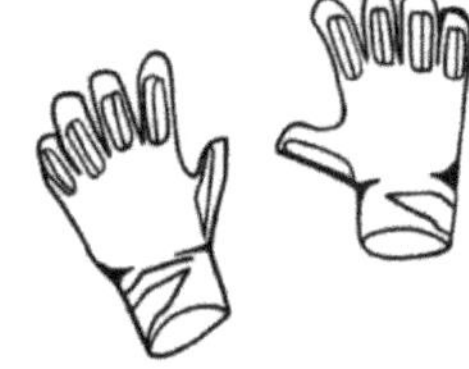

Check out our Sprinkle Joy Publishing Book, *The Champ*.

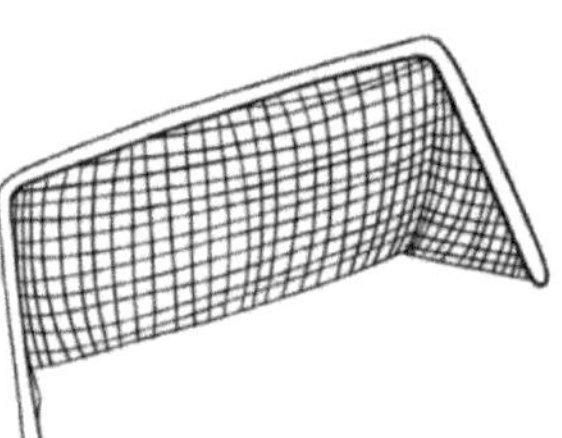
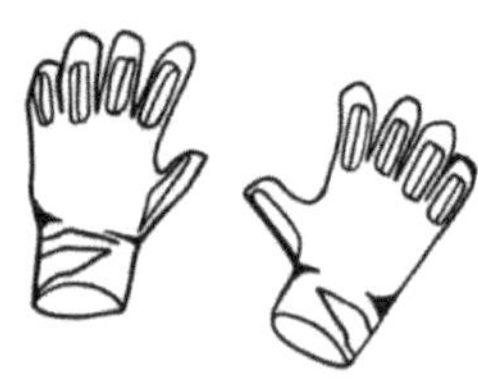

Amari and Aida SOCCER Coloring & Activity Workbook for Kids!

Written by
Carline Constant and Gregory Constant

Sprinkle Joy
Publishing

My name is Amari. I love to play soccer.
I am a great player and live for kicking the ball.
My favorite part is scoring goals!

My name is Aida. I enjoy playing soccer.
Kicking the ball and scoring goals is so much fun!

Grandpa says, "Amari, soccer is not just about you.
It takes more than one person to make a team. You
and Aida must play the game together."

Even though I don't
like it, I want Grandpa
to see that I can partner
up. I pass the ball to
Aida on the opposite
side of the field.

I run alongside Aida, she's almost as fast as I am. Grandpa runs to her and steals the ball. Aida waves for me to cover the side of the field where Grandpa now has the ball. I nod to her. Together, we block Grandpa and take the ball. Grandpa calls out, "I see the two of you have become a dynamic duo!" We burst into laughter.

With a firm kick, Aida sends the ball flying
into the net.
It goes in! "G-O-A-L! G-O-O-O-O-A-A-L!"
Aida runs around the field
with her arms wide open.

"Teamwork pays off!"
We're grateful to have Grandpa here to teach us.

ROUTINE ACTIVITY
Soccer Exercise

Your body needs at least 60 minutes of exercise each day.
Playing soccer is a good way to get exercise.
Ask a parent, grandparent, teacher, or sibling to join you in
playing soccer for fun exercise!

Directions: Use the soccer vocabulary words below to complete the puzzle down and across.

CROSSWORD PUZZLE

Across

2. _____________ is a team sport, known as football around the world.

3. _____________ is showing respect towards the game and other players.

6. A group of people working together is called a _____________

Down

1. Your body needs 60 minutes of _____________ per day.

4. It's _____________ when you work with a group of people to achieve a goal.

5. A person taking part in a sports event is a _____________

Soccer Vocabulary Words.

Exercise	Player	Soccer	Sportsmanship	Team	Teamwork

Soccer Crossword Puzzle

Across

3. ______________ is guarding a player closely to prevent him or her from advancing the ball towards the net from a teammate.

6. The _________ is the player positioned in front of the goal who tries to prevent shots from getting into the net.

7. The official governing organization of international soccer, they set and revise rules of the game. It's called ___________.

8. Bringing the ball under control _________ it using the foot, thigh, chest or head.

10. A ball kicked or headed by a player ___________ towards the opponent's goal to score.

Down

1. When the player ___________ he advances the ball with his feet while controlling it.

2. Players that play in front are ___________ of the team and are responsible for taking most of the shots on goal.

4. The only player allowed to use his hands and arms is the ___________.

5. The striking of a ball in the air by a player's head is a __________.

9. A player kicks the ball to __________ pass it to her teammate.

Soccer Vocabulary Words.

| FIFA | Goalie | Shot | Dribble | Trap | GoalKeeper | Forward | Marking | Header | Pass |

Search For The Words

```
F  O  E  P  L  A  Y  E  R  O  R  D  X  J  X
Q  I  T  F  L  D  W  M  N  P  C  K  G  R  W
M  M  F  E  D  W  S  W  D  S  Q  C  E  S  N
Q  L  P  A  A  O  O  P  A  P  S  Q  X  R  G
G  Q  E  R  P  M  C  N  T  O  K  R  E  M  O
N  P  L  A  R  Q  C  A  L  R  W  M  R  P  A
I  E  P  O  N  M  E  C  F  T  H  G  C  E  L
T  E  A  M  W  O  R  K  C  S  U  Q  I  R  K
R  S  H  E  A  D  E  R  C  M  N  U  S  G  E
A  A  X  P  A  W  V  D  I  A  L  A  E  G  E
M  P  L  I  R  G  G  J  J  N  P  O  R  P  P
X  O  L  M  T  O  S  D  G  S  B  V  T  R  E
X  Z  P  O  Q  W  L  T  N  H  B  L  C  E  R
Z  C  H  Q  W  P  A  G  F  I  N  O  E  Q  R
W  S  T  R  Q  F  O  R  W  P  R  D  T  L  D
```

SOCCER   PLAYER   TEAM

TEAMWORK   SPORTSMANSHIP   EXERCISE

Find the Word in the Puzzle
Words can go in any direction.
Words can share letters as they cross over each other.

Soccer Scramble Word Search

```
F  O  E  F  L  T  R  A  P  O  R  D  X  J  X
Q  I  X  F  L  D  W  M  N  P  C  K  G  R  W
M  M  F  H  D  W  P  W  D  M  Q  C  O  S  N
Q  L  P  A  N  O  F  P  A  S  S  Q  A  R  G
G  Q  E  R  P  L  C  N  T  J  K  R  L  M  O
N  P  L  A  R  Q  P  A  L  R  W  M  I  P  A
I  E  P  O  N  M  B  C  F  P  H  G  E  E  L
K  B  J  D  N  R  D  B  C  D  U  Q  M  R  K
R  S  H  E  A  D  E  R  C  V  N  U  Q  G  E
A  A  X  P  A  W  V  D  I  S  L  A  K  G  E
M  P  L  I  R  G  G  J  J  B  P  O  R  P  P
X  O  L  M  T  O  S  D  G  P  B  V  T  R  E
X  Z  P  O  Q  W  L  T  N  A  B  L  C  E  R
Z  C  H  Q  W  P  A  G  F  M  N  O  E  Q  R
W  S  T  R  Q  F  O  R  W  A  R  D  T  L  D
```

dribble	FIFA	forward
goalie	goalkeeper	header
marking	pass	shot
trap		

Find the Word in the Puzzle

Words can go in any direction.
Words can share letters as they cross over each other.

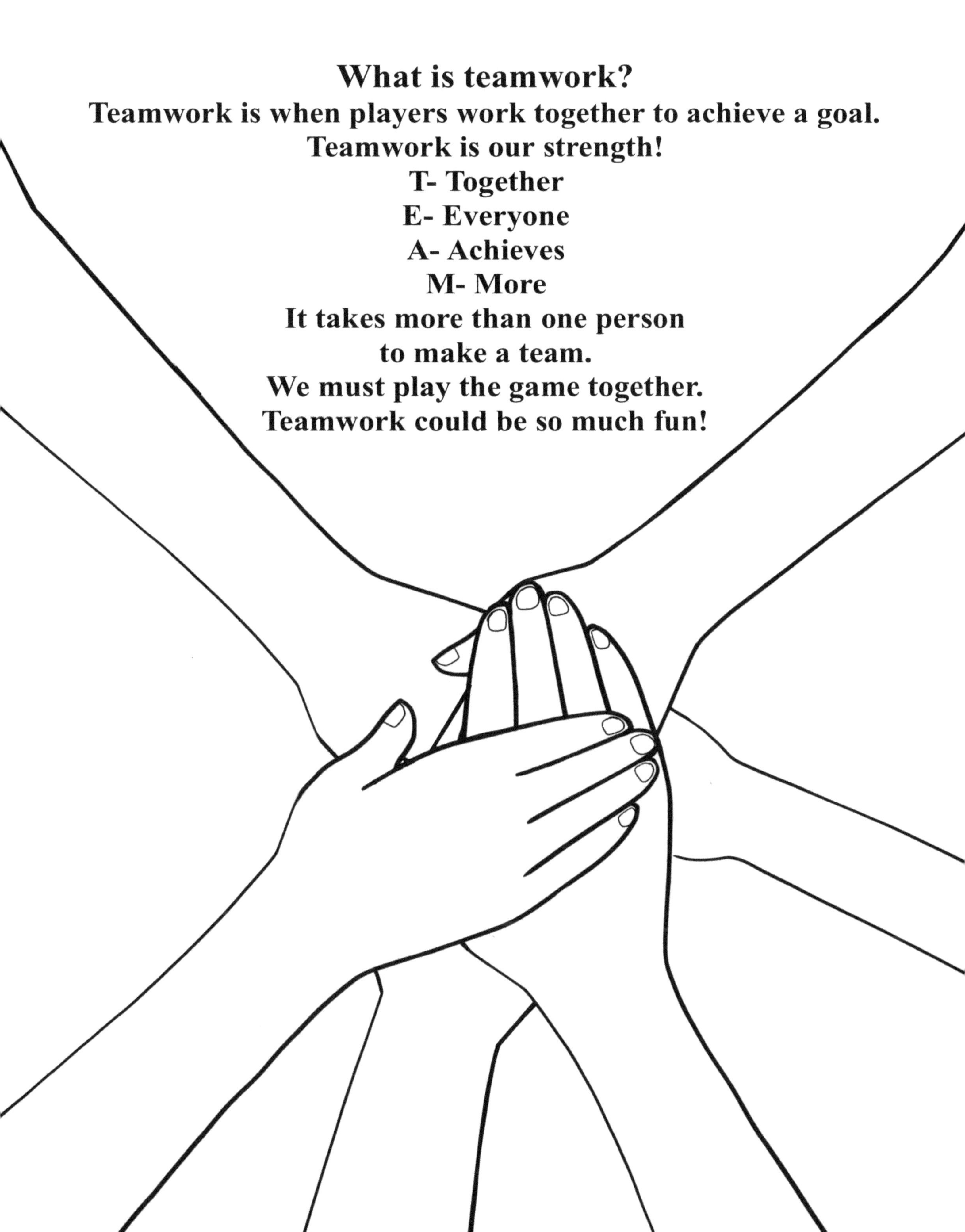
What is teamwork?
Teamwork is when players work together to achieve a goal.
Teamwork is our strength!
T- Together
E- Everyone
A- Achieves
M- More
It takes more than one person
to make a team.
We must play the game together.
Teamwork could be so much fun!

My Favorite Soccer Player

Have a parent, grandparent, guardian, teacher, or older sibling help you.

Directions: Choose, circle a soccer player's name below before writing. Write about your favorite soccer player, write the name of the country and draw the flag.

Men Soccer Players

-Messi -MBappe -Pele -Maradona -Cristiano Ronaldo
-Neymar -Ronaldo -Ronaldinho -Romario -Beckman
-Best -Henry -Zidane -Modric -Saka -Kane -Cruyff

Women Soccer Players

-Alex Morgan -Mia Hamm -Lucy Bronze -Pernille Harder
-Alexia Putellas -Jo Si-Yun -Wendie Renard -Lindsey Horan
-Vivianne Mieder -Rose Lavelle -Amandine Henry

____

My favorite soccer player is _________________ because

____
____
____
The name of the country this soccer player is from is ___________

Draw the flag below:

ACTIVITY: **KIDS OF CHARACTER**

Directions: Talk to a parent, grandparent, guardian, teacher or older sibling about the Kid of Character Vocabulary words below. Together, work on building your character.

*Place a check ✅ next to each number if you're a kid of character.

Vocabulary: **Respect, self-control, kind, responsibility, cooperating, helpful.**

1. By using my manners, I show respect to people. ————

2. I have self-control over my behavior by not always showing that I am angry.————

3. I am kind when I care for others. ————

4. I know that completing my homework and helping others is responsibility.————

5. When I recycle items, I know that's helpful for the environment.————

6. I work together cooperating with my teammates, taking turns and sharing.————

REMEMBER: Teamwork is when players work together to achieve a goal.
What are some ways you can show teamwork in sports?

____

____

____

____

You are a SOCCER STAR! You can design or make a soccer jersey for your team or yourself!

(Ask a parent/guardian/teacher or sibling to help you.)

Directions:

1) Create soccer jerseys using the following templates.

2) Choose a number and write it on the front of the soccer jerseys. Be sure to write your name.

3) Use your favorite colors of crayons, markers or pencils to decorate the soccer jerseys.

These soccer jerseys belong to: _________________, a soccer star!

ROUTINE SOCCER ACTIVITIES- MATH CHALLENGE

$9 + 8 =$ _____

$529 + 93 = 6 \triangle 2$

$7 \times$ _____ $= 56$

$9 + 5 \triangle 18 - 5$
(choose one =, < , >)

$83 \times 4 =$ _____

$42 + 4 =$ _____

$85 + 6 =$ _____

$465 -$ _____ $= 73$

$21 \div 4 =$ _____

$372 \div 6 =$ _____

Draw an array for 3 x 5 on the line that follows

____

Make Your Own Soccer Team

Mark your position on the soccer field and show your way to the winning goal.

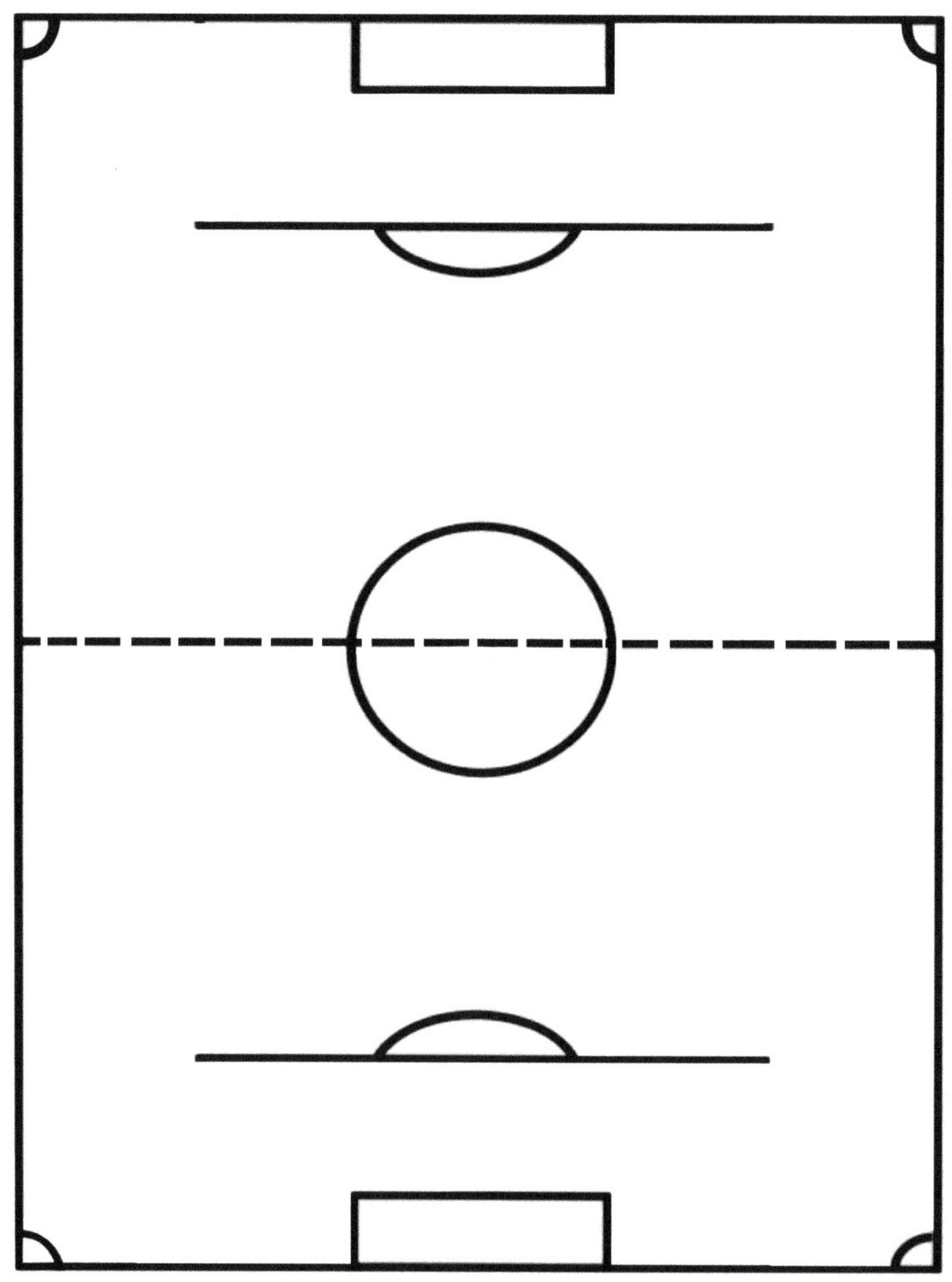

Color in your Soccer Jerseys and add a number to each.

Soccer Word Problems - Routine Math Challenge

Directions: Read each problem and solve to find the answer.
Show your work.

1. How many soccer balls would you have if you had 22 bags of
   soccer balls with 17 soccer balls in each bag?

2. Aida and Grandpa picked 45 soccer balls from the community
   fields in a week. Her brother Amari picked 9 soccer balls from the
   school yard in 7 days. How many times as many soccer balls did
   Aida and Grandpa pick?

3. In the park, over 6 months, Amari and Aida saw 23 dogs.
   How many legs did they see?

4. Grandpa ordered 7 pepperoni pizzas and 5 extra cheese pizzas for
   the team after the soccer game. Each pizza has 8 slices. How
   many slices are there all together?

5. How many groups of 3 can be made from 27 soccer balls?

Color in your soccer jersey and add a number.

This is my favorite team Soccer Jersey.

Color the back of of the jersey and add your name and number.

Soccer Prize:

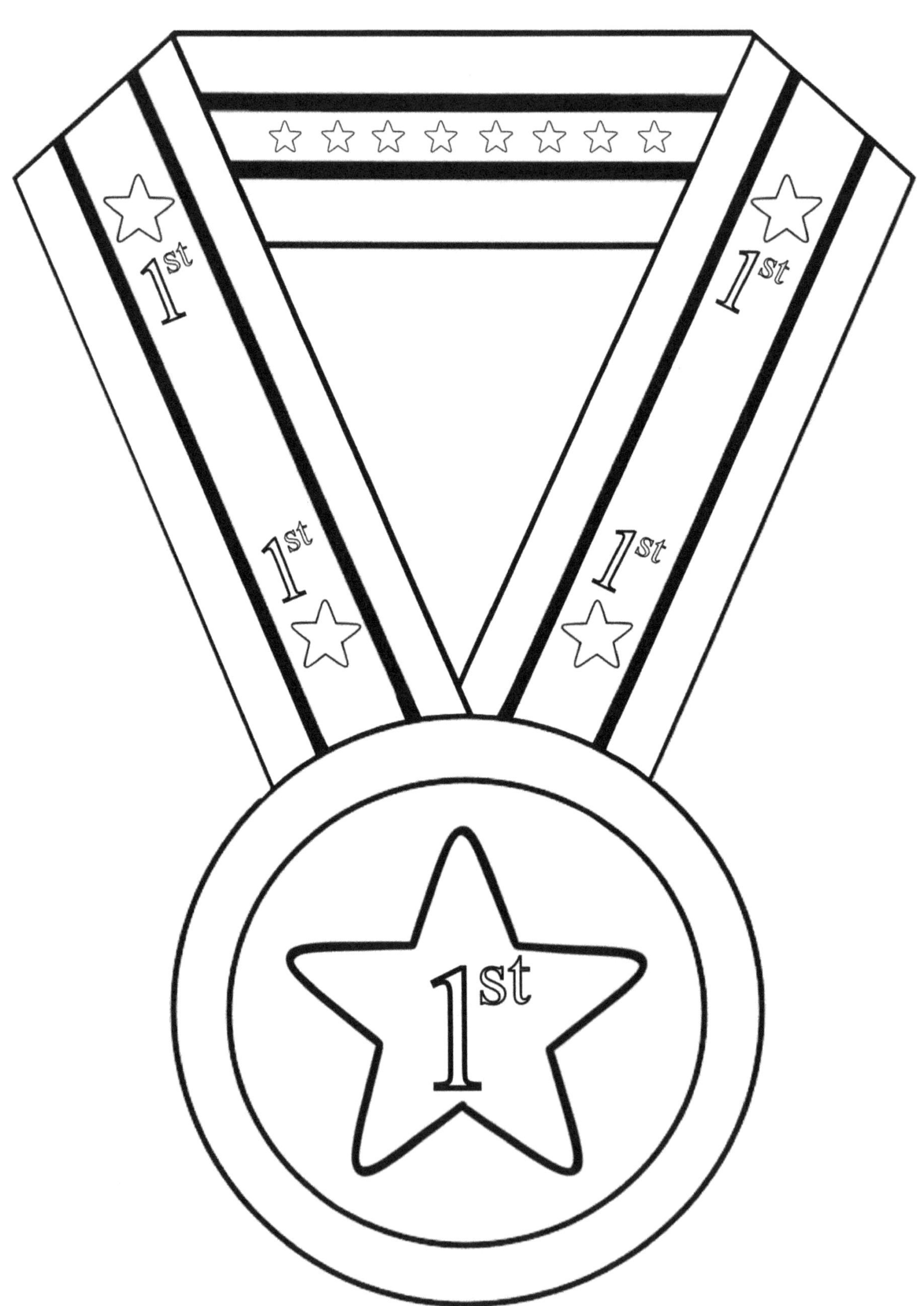

PHONICS

Vowel Sounds
<u>Directions</u>: Have a parent, grandparent, guardian, teacher, or older sibling help you. After saying the first word in each box, be sure to repeat it. Carefully say each word on the same line. Circle the words that make the same vowel sound as the fist word. Don't be tricked!

1. <u>ball</u>-   strap   crawl   mall   haul

2. <u>play</u>-   layer   day   happy   survey

3. <u>team</u>-   let   beam   dine   lean

4. <u>prize</u>-   nip   rise   give   eyes

5. <u>press</u>-   jets   feast   bless   sweats

6. <u>School</u>-   cool   crop   pool   views

7. <u>action</u>-   caption   education   imagine   happen

8. <u>people</u>-   cable   police   above   sequel

9. <u>together</u>-   eater   mother   feather   liver

10. <u>dribble</u>-   people   Sybil   drip   scribble

PHONICS

<u>Directions</u>: Look and trace the pictures in the box.

<u>Say</u> the words -

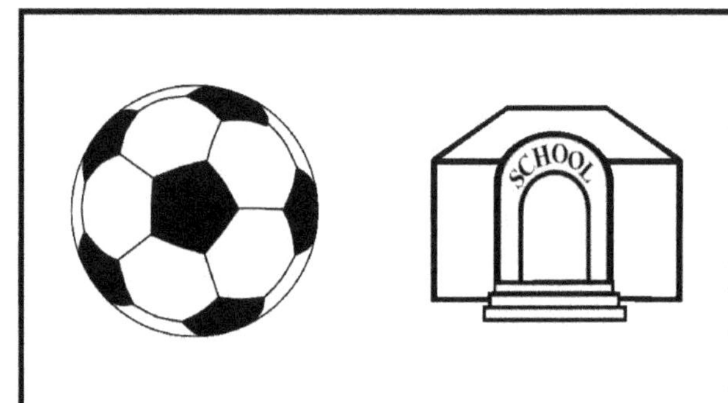

ball   ball   ball

school   school   school

<u>Trace</u> the words -

ball   ball   ball   ball

school   school   school   school

<u>Write sentences with</u> the words on the line below.

____

____

____

____

<u>Identify, say and Circle</u> the words: -ball -school

-boil   -all   -ball   -fall   -bail   -ball

-pool   -school   -schorl   -hoop   -scholar   -school

 # PHONICS 

PHONICS PRACTICE
<u>Directions</u>: Read and break up the compound words, for example - pop/corn.
Sound out and write the compound words on the line.
If the word is not compound words, place an (X) on the line next to it.
*Remember that compound words are two simple words that make up one word
(popcorn = pop/corn)

1. mailbox _______________________________

2. afternoon _______________________________

3. eyesight _______________________________

4. pocket _______________________________

5. magnet _______________________________

6. goldfish _______________________________

Write some other **compound words** that you know in the box below.

 # PHONICS 

Words to spell, read and write.

Directions: Spell and read the words below. Create your own phonics list by completing the chart with group of words that have the same vowel sound as the first word.

The first line is an example.

/a/	/e/	/i/	/o/	/u/
cat	net	win	fog	fun
hat	___	___	___	___
___	___	___	___	___
___	___	___	___	___
___	___	___	___	___
___	___	___	___	___

PHONICS

PHONICS

Words to spell, read and write.

<u>Directions:</u> Read, spell and write sentences using the words below. Place the words on index cards for practice.

/qu/ ('kw')

quack   The ducks on the farm go quack, quack all day long.

quest   _______________________________

quick   _______________________________

quill   _______________________________

quilt   _______________________________

squid   _______________________________

Soccer Ball

Cleats

Best
Goal

Name : ---

Team Name : ---

Date : ---

Best GoalKeeper
to
Name : ---
Team Name : -------------------------------------
Date : --

Make your own bookmarks

Create bookmarks by drawing and writing scenes from the story "The Champ."

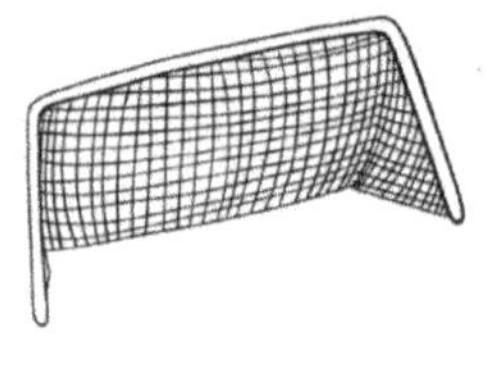

SOCCER RESOURCES

Readers with parental/guardian consent, for more soccer information, log on to our Sprinkle Joy Books website at https://www.sprinklejoybooks.com under our Newsletter tag for free soccer resources.

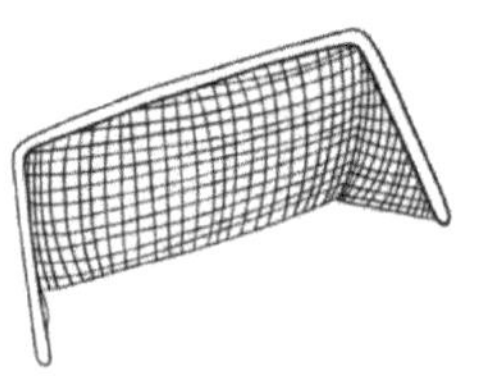

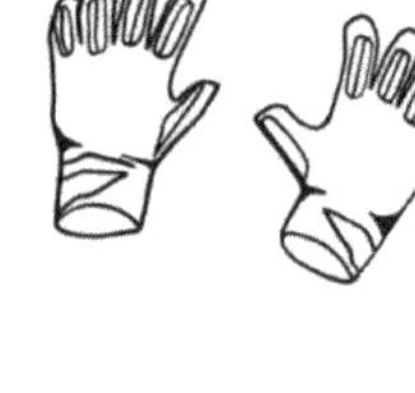

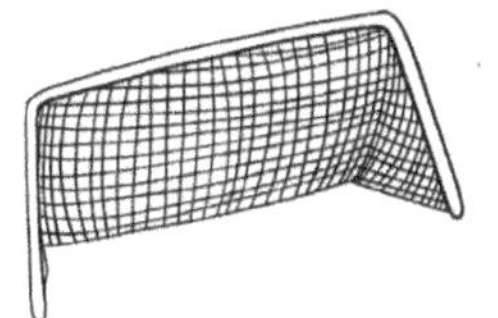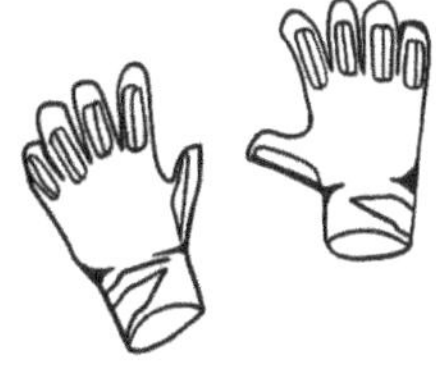

Thank you for your purchase!
If you enjoyed this coloring & activity workbook,
please leave a review.
We read every review and
they help new readers discover our workbooks.

Check out our Sprinkle Joy Publishing Book, *The Champ*.

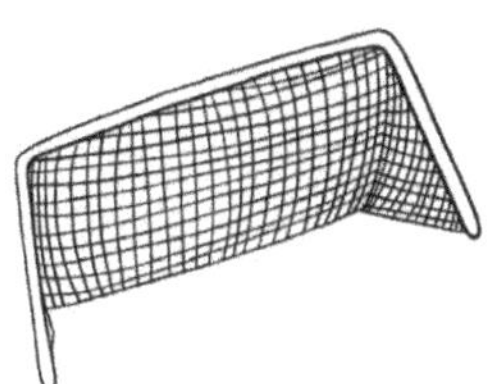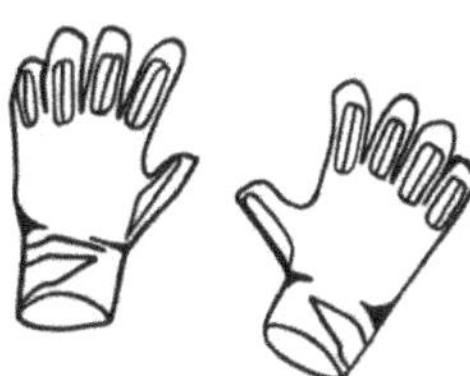